The Very Noisy Night

Diana Hendry   Jane Chapman

THE TRAVELLING BOOK COMPANY

D1408622

It was the middle of the night and Big Mouse was fast asleep in his big bed. Little Mouse was wide awake in his little bed.
"Big Mouse! Big Mouse!" called Little Mouse.
"I can hear something rushing round the house, huffing and puffing."

Big Mouse opened one eye and one ear.
"It's only the wind," he said.

"Can I come into your bed?" asked Little Mouse.
"No," said Big Mouse. "There isn't room."
And he turned over and went back to sleep.

Little Mouse lay listening
to the wind. Then, suddenly,
between a huff and a puff,
came a . . .

TAP TAP *TAP*

TAP

Little Mouse climbed out of bed,
opened the front door — just
a crack — and peeped out.

WHOOOSH!

went the wind, but there was no one outside. "Big Mouse! Big Mouse!" called Little Mouse. "I can hear someone tapping. Perhaps there's a burglar on the roof."

Big Mouse got out of bed and opened the bedroom curtains. "Look," he said, "it's only a branch tapping on the window. Go back to sleep."
"Can I come into your bed?" asked Little Mouse.
"No," said Big Mouse. "You wriggle."

Little Mouse lay in his own bed and listened to the wind huffing and puffing and the branch tap-tapping — and someone calling,

"HOO-HOO! HOO-HOO!"

Little Mouse climbed out of bed again. This time he looked under it. Then he looked in the wardrobe, and feeling very frightened he cried, "Big Mouse! Big Mouse! I think there's a ghost in the house, and it's looking for me. It keeps calling, who-who, who-who?"

Big Mouse sighed, sat up
and listened. "It's only an owl,"
he said. "It's awake, like you."
"Can I come into your bed?"
asked Little Mouse.
"No," said Big Mouse. "Your
paws are always cold."
And Big Mouse pulled the
blanket over his head and
went back to sleep.

Little Mouse got back into his own
bed and he lay and listened
to the wind huffing and
puffing, the branch
tap-tapping, and
the owl hooting.
But sssh!
What was that?

"Big Mouse! Big Mouse!" he called. "I think it's raining inside." And Little Mouse jumped out of bed and fetched his red umbrella.

Big Mouse got out of bed too. He opened the front door.
"Be quiet, wind," he said. "Be quiet, branch. Be quiet, owl."
But they took no notice. Then Big Mouse turned off the
dripping tap and put away the umbrella.

"Can I come into your bed?"
asked Little Mouse.
"No, you're nice and snug in your own bed,"
said Big Mouse, taking him back to the bedroom.

Little Mouse lay and
listened to the wind
huffing and puffing,
the branch tap-tapping,
and the owl hooting.
And just as he was
beginning to feel very
sleepy indeed, he heard . . .

"WHEEE,
WHEEE,
WHEEEEE!"

"Big Mouse! Big Mouse!"
he called. "You're snoring."

Wearily Big Mouse
got up. He put his
ear-muffs on Little
Mouse's ears.
He put a paper-clip
on his own nose, and
he went back to bed.

Little Mouse lay and listened to — n o t h i n g !
It was very, very, very quiet. He couldn't hear
the wind huffing or the branch tapping or the owl
hooting or Big Mouse snoring. It was so quiet that
Little Mouse felt he was all alone in the world.

He took off the ear-muffs. He got out of bed
and pulled the paper-clip off Big Mouse's nose.
"Big Mouse! Big Mouse!" he cried, "I'm lonely!"

Big Mouse flung back
his blanket. "Better come
into my bed," he said.
So Little Mouse hopped
in and his paws were
cold . . .

and he needed just
a little wriggle before
he fell fast asleep.

Big Mouse lay and listened to the wind huffing and puffing and the branch tapping and the owl hooting and Little Mouse snuffling, and very soon he heard the birds waking up. But neither of them heard the alarm clock . . .

. . . BECAUSE THEY WERE
BOTH FAST ASLEEP!

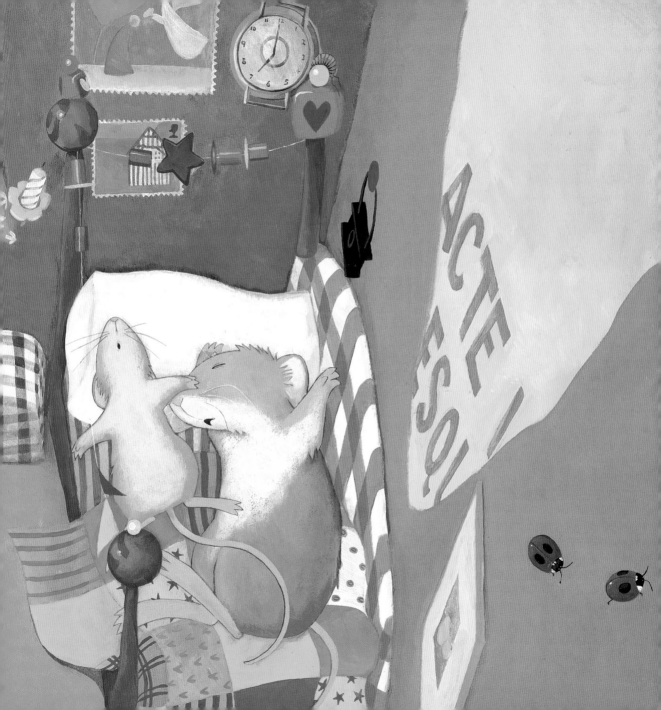

For Emelia, with love
— D.H.

For Anthony, Jane, Mark,
Katy and Alice, with love
— J.C.

LITTLE TIGER PRESS
An imprint of Magi Publications
1 The Coda Centre, 189 Munster Road, London SW6 6AW
www.littletigerpress.com
First published in Great Britain 1999
This edition published 2007
Text © Diana Hendry, 1999 · Illustrations © Jane Chapman, 1999
Diana Hendry and Jane Chapman have asserted their rights to be identified as the
author and illustrator of this work under the Copyright, Designs and Patents Act, 1988
All rights reserved
ISBN 978-1-84506-522-5 • Printed in China
4 6 8 10 9 7 5 3